THIS BIG HERO 6 ANNUAL 2016

belongs to

....

....

.... Write your name here.

BIG HERO 6

ANNUAL 2016

CONTENTS

EGMONT
We bring stories to life

First published in 2015 by Egmont UK Limited,
1 Nicholas Road, London W11 4AN

Activities and story adaptation by Brenda Apsley.
Design by Jeannette O'Toole.
Created for Egmont UK Limited by Ruby Shoes Limited.
© 2015 Disney Enterprises, Inc.

ISBN 978 1 4052 7866 9
61457/1

Stay safe online. Any website addresses listed in this book
are correct at the time of going to print. However, Egmont
is not responsible for content hosted by third parties.
Please be aware that online content can be subject
to change and websites can contain content that
is unsuitable for children. We advise that all children
are supervised when using the internet.

BIG HERO 6

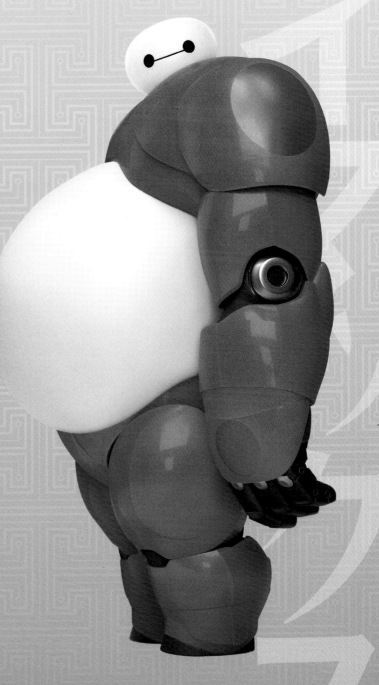

TOGETHER WE'RE ...
UNBEATABLE!

SAY HI TO THE HAMADAS

HIRO HAMADA. You could call him a geek. You could call him a techie. Or even a bit of a nerd.

What you should call him is a massively intelligent brainiac. He may be only fourteen years old, but he has already graduated from high school at the age of just thirteen (and that's YOUNG!). **THEY COULDN'T TEACH HIM ANYTHING HE DIDN'T ALREADY KNOW!**

Thanks to Hiro's mega-brainpower and confidence, he's a walking talking prodigy who has the skills, knowledge and ideas of someone much older.

Hiro loves robotics, and designs and makes his own incredibly powerful fighting robots. The thing he likes best is taking them to secret bot fights, pitting them against the best bots out there – and **WINNING!**

BIG BRAIN

TADASHI HAMADA is Hiro's big brother and the person Hiro looks up to more than any other. Tadashi is a top robotics student at San Fransokyo Institute of Technology, and he takes his studies very seriously — unlike Hiro, who'd rather HAVE FUN THAN STUDY.

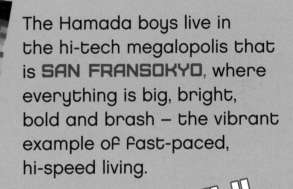

TOP STUDENT

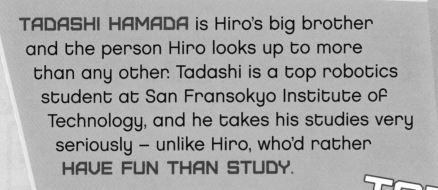

The Hamada boys live in the hi-tech megalopolis that is SAN FRANSOKYO, where everything is big, bright, bold and brash — the vibrant example of fast-paced, hi-speed living.

MEGA CITY!

The brothers live with their AUNT CASS in an apartment above the coffee shop she owns and runs. It's a buzzing, popular place called the LUCKY CAT CAFE.
The lucky cat Aunt Cass's cafe is named after is MOCHI, who thinks that HE owns and runs the place. He's a real control-cat.

MEOWW!

9

CHAPTER 1

HIRO HAMADA was fourteen, but had the mega-brain and techno skills of someone much older.

He had graduated from high school super-early, and now spent his time designing and building vicious fighting robots like **MEGABOT**. He pitted it against other fighting bots in secret backstreet fights – and won.

Hiro's big brother, Tadashi, didn't approve of bot fights. "A genius like you could change the world," he said. "You should use your big brain, and attend college with me."

Hiro shrugged. He was still a kid, and he liked bot fights, no, he **LOVED** bot fights. **SCHOOL COULD WAIT.**

When Hiro found out about the next bot fight, he was surprised when Tadashi offered to give him a lift there.

On the way, though, Tadashi stopped at his college, SFIT, the San Fransokyo Institute of Technology.

In the amazing, super-hi-tech lab, Tadashi stuck a piece of tape on Hiro's arm and ripped it off again, complete with hairs!

That hurt! "**OW!**" shouted Hiro.

サンフランソーキョー

SF

ヒロ

ベイマックス

His cry of pain made a suitcase open up, and a robot inflated from inside.

"HELLO, I AM BAYMAX, YOUR PERSONAL HEALTH CARE COMPANION," said the robot as it diagnosed Hiro's sore arm, and soothed his pain.

Tadashi smiled. He showed Hiro a green nurse chip he had fitted inside the robot's access port on his chest, and explained how it worked. "I programmed him with over 10,000 medical procedures and a special care-giving interface that makes Baymax ..." He paused, searching for the right word. "That makes Baymax ... well, Baymax!"

The robot spoke to Hiro again.

"I CANNOT DEACTIVATE UNTIL YOU SAY YOU ARE SATISFIED WITH YOUR CARE."

Now it was Hiro's turn to smile. "Well, I am satisfied with my care," he said, and he touched Baymax's hand, the nearest he could get to shaking hands with a robot.

When Tadashi's robotics teacher, Professor Robert Callaghan, arrived, he took a look at Megabot. "Impressive," he said, then he paused. "Have you thought of studying here? **MY STUDENTS GO ON TO SHAPE THE FUTURE.**"

WOW! Suddenly, Hiro was ready to go back to school!

"Enter the showcase," Tadashi told him. "Invent something to impress the judges and they'll give you a place."

Hiro worked like crazy, and at the showcase he presented his **MICROBOTS**, tiny robots he controlled with his thoughts via a neural transmitter in his headband. They swarmed together to make whatever he imagined: bridges, skyscrapers – anything!

The Microbots got Hiro his place, and an offer from Alistair Krei of Krei Tech to buy them, but he refused to sell.

Later, as Hiro and Tadashi left, people ran by, screaming, "FIRE! FIRE!"

Tadashi ran inside to help when – KABOOM! – there was a huge explosion. "Tadashi, NOOOOO!" screamed Hiro. But Tadashi was gone ...

SAY HI TO TADASHI'S FRIENDS

When Tadashi took Hiro to his college he introduced him to his fellow students in the SFIT lab, and they showed him their latest projects. He was seriously impressed!

ゴーゴートマゴ

GO-GO TOMAGO

is a mechanical engineer of few words, but she lets her work do the talking for her. She is tough, athletic, and sometimes a bit sarcastic, but she's also super-loyal to her friends. Her current project was a superfast mag-lev bicycle.

Hiro's verdict:
"AWESOME!"

Physics ace **WASABI NO-GINGER** loves the planning, precision and organisation that goes into his specialist area: laser technology. He was working hard at his bench, which was littered with tools, on a laser just half a micron wide. That's infinitessimally small.

"ALMOST IMPOSSIBLE!"
said Hiro.

ワサビ

ハニーレモン

Upbeat chemistry wizard **HONEY LEMON** is the talker of the group. "Omigosh! Perfect timing, you guys! You're just gonna love this!" Test tube in hand, she couldn't wait to show off her latest experiment and seconds later her chemical concoction completely disintegrated a huge ball of metal!

What could Hiro say?
"OMIGOSH!"

Tadashi's fourth friend is **FRED**, who seemed to do ... well, not much at all, unless you count watching movies and reading comic books as work. Truth is, good-natured, laid-back Fred doesn't do a lot of anything, but he does like to hang out with smart people – and they don't get any smarter than the lab geeks at SFIT.

Hiro appreciated that.
"SMART GUY!"

フレッド"

THE NEXT BIG BOT FIGHT

Hiro loves bot fights, but the police don't. So when a new fight is planned, it's always at a top secret destination in the back streets of San Fransokyo.

Details of the location go out in a series of coded directions, and the fighters – and their bots – follow the clues until they reach the fight site.

Where is the next bot fight? Starting in section **1A**, follow the number and direction code at the top of page 19, moving from square to square

UP ↑
DOWN ↓
LEFT ←
RIGHT →

Which map section is the next fight in? Write the number and letter.

9 10 11 12 13 14 15 16 17 18 19 20

Answer on page 68.

CODE BREAKER

Can you draw in the symbols that complete the code square so that each one appears only **ONCE** in each line across and down?

国	米		
	モ		国
米			モ
	国	ツ	

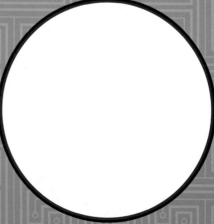

ON A SCALE OF 1 TO 10, how do you rate your code-breaking skills? Draw a face to show your score.

 1   2   3   4   5

 6   7   8   9   10

Answers on page 68.

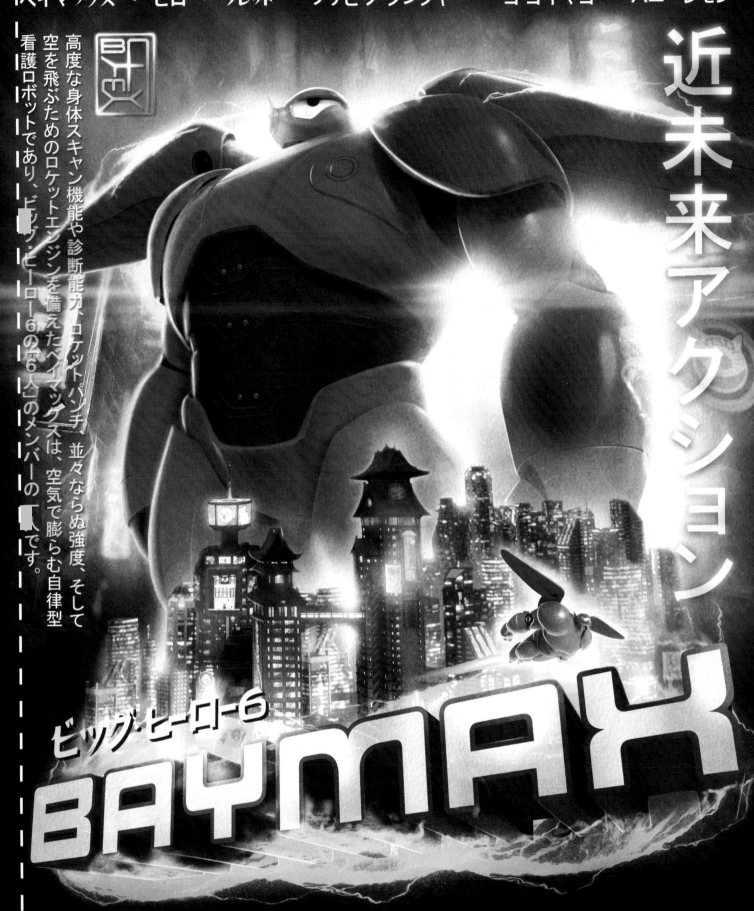

SAN FRANSOKYO

WOW! The megalopolis that is San Fransokyo is one awesome city!

Which of these details can you see in the cityscape?
Tick ✔ the ones you can see and cross ✘ the ones you can't.

A

B

C

D

E

F

G

H

I

Answers on page 68.

23

WHAT DO YOU KNOW? PART 1

Try answering these questions about the story so far.

1 Hiro lives in San Fernando. True or false?
Write a tick ✔ for true or a cross ✗ for false.

2 How old is Hiro? Write the number.

3 What is the name of Hiro's fighting robot?

5 What does Professor Robert Callaghan teach?

4 What is Hiro's big brother called? Tick ✔ a box.

A Tamishi

B Tadashi

C Tomiki

6 What do the letters SFIT stand for? Tick ✔ a box.

A San Francisco Institute of Television

B San Fransokyo Institute of Technology

C San Francis Institute of Theatre

7 Aunt Cass's coffee shop is called the Lucky Cat Cafe. True or false? Write a tick ✔ for true or a cross ✘ for false.

8 What colour chip did Tadashi fit in his health care robot, Baymax? Tick ✔ a colour.

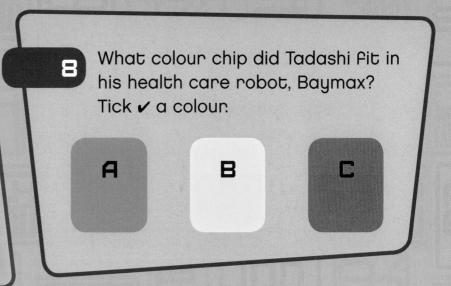

A B C

9 "HELLO, I AM _ _ _ _ _ _ _ , YOUR

PERSONAL _ _ _ _ _ _ CARE COMPANION."

Can you fill in the 2 missing words?

10 Hiro controls his microbots with a neural transmitter he wears – where? Tick ✔ a box.

A wristband B headband

C hoodie

Check your answers on page 68.

ON A SCALE OF 1 TO 10, how many questions did you get right? Draw a face to show your score.

 1
 2
 3
4
5

 6
 7
 8
 9
 10

SAY HI TO BAYMAX

You just have to love Baymax! He's a soft, squishy, over-inflated, extra-huggable white bag-of-air robot who has only one aim in life: **THE CARE AND WELLBEING OF OTHERS.**

Tadashi Hamada created him in the robotics lab at SFIT as something new and very different: a walking talking portable medical aid he called a **NURSE-BOT.**

Tadashi fitted a special green nurse chip into the access port on Baymax's chest, and programmed him with 10,000 medical procedures and a unique care-giving interface.

When he hears a cry of pain, Baymax inflates out of the suitcase where he's kept, scans the patient to find out what's wrong, sorts out the problem – and soothes the pain.

When you hear the words, **"HELLO, I AM BAYMAX, YOUR PERSONAL HEALTH CARE COMPANION,"** you know you're in good hands and will get expert care!

When he asks, **"ARE YOU SATISFIED WITH YOUR CARE?"** there's only one possible answer – a great big **YES!**

When Hiro met him and needed help, he soon realised that Baymax could be so much more than a care-giver and best friend – he could be a **HERO**!

Baymax would really love to play with one of Hiro's footballs. But he's so springy and bouncy and over-inflated with air that as soon as he touches them, they roll away. **ON A SCALE OF ONE TO TEN,** how annoying is that?

Count all the footballs and write the number.

footballs

One ball is different from the rest. Can you find it?

Answers on page 68.

WHAT COMES NEXT?

Activate your brain power!
Can you draw in what comes next in each sequence?

1 国 米 国 米 国 ◻

2 モ ツ モ ツ モ ◻

3 国 米 国 国 米 ◻

4 ワ 文野 ヒロ ワ 文野 ◻

5 光 光 国 国 光 ◻

Answers on page 68.

MICROBOTS!

Skyscrapers, bridges, airships: using the power of his thoughts, Hiro can form his microbots into just about anything!

Use your imagination and dream up ... whatever your thoughts decide! Draw or doodle your microbot creation, then write a title and your name.

....

BY ....

After Tadashi's death, Hiro felt very alone. With his big brother gone, nothing seemed to matter anymore. Days passed, then weeks, and still Hiro sat in his room.

One day he was holding Megabot when part of the robot detached and landed on his toe – hard.

"OUCH!" cried Hiro.

"HELLO, I AM BAYMAX, YOUR PERSONAL HEALTH CARE COMPANION," said a voice he had heard before. Hiro's cry of pain had activated Tadashi's robot, Baymax!

As Hiro watched, the big white nurse robot inflated little by little and emerged from his suitcase.

ベイマックス

"ON A SCALE OF 1 TO 10, HOW WOULD YOU RATE YOUR PAIN?" Baymax asked Hiro.

Hiro didn't answer, and he made it very clear that there was no way he would be scanned.

"I CANNOT DEACTIVATE UNTIL YOU SAY YOU ARE SATISFIED WITH YOUR CARE," said Baymax.

"FINE!" cried Hiro. He backed away, tripped, fell, and found himself looking under his bed at the hoodie he'd worn at the SFIT showcase. In its pocket was the microbot Alistair Krei had been holding. "Dumb thing must be broken," said Hiro, putting it in a dish, where it buzzed angrily.

ヒロ

 "YOUR TINY ROBOT IS TRYING TO GO SOMEWHERE," said Baymax as the microbot banged against the dish.

"OH YEAH?" said Hiro, turning away. "Then why don't you find out where it's trying to go?"

Seconds later Hiro heard a squeal of tyres outside, and ran to the window. Baymax was outside, in the middle of the manic city traffic! He couldn't let anything happen to his brother's robot, and raced outside.

Baymax followed the microbot's directions, and Hiro followed Baymax, catching up with him outside an old warehouse.

"I HAVE FOUND OUT WHERE YOUR TINY ROBOT WANTS TO GO," Baymax told him.

Yes, the microbot was pointing at the warehouse!

Hiro and Baymax found an open window and climbed inside, and Hiro gasped at what he saw: MICROBOTS! THOUSANDS AND THOUSANDS OF THEM! And more were spilling on to a conveyor belt. Someone was making them – LOTS of them. But who?

He found out when the microbots swarmed angrily and attacked them, controlled by a man in a long black coat and a red and white mask.

Hiro and Baymax ran, and the microbot swarm pushed them back out of the window.

34

Baymax was low on energy and filled with holes from the microbots' sharp edges, so Hiro took him home and put him on his charging station.

"TADASHI," said Baymax.

Hiro sighed. "Tadashi's dead."

Baymax filtered the information, scanned Hiro and gave his diagnosis: GRIEF. But there was no treatment for that in his database, so he downloaded info from Hiro's computer.

PROBLEM: LOSS OF A LOVED ONE.

TREATMENT: CONTACT WITH FRIENDS AND LOVED ONES.

Baymax called the lab guys and gave Hiro a big robot-size hug. "I AM SORRY ABOUT THE FIRE," he said.

"It's okay," said Hiro. "It was an accident." But WAS it? NO, Hiro suddenly realised that THE MASKED MAN STOLE THE MICROBOTS AND STARTED THE FIRE!

"We gotta catch that guy," said Hiro, and he started working to **UPGRADE BAYMAX TO A FIGHTING ROBOT.** He created armour with his 3D printer, and put a red fighting chip in his chest, next to Tadashi's green nurse chip.

With his new look and new armour, Baymax was ready to fight, and he and Hiro went back to the warehouse to face the masked man, who called himself **YOKAI**.

Outside, they came face to face with a massive swarm of microbots – and Yokai. **THEY WERE IN TROUBLE!**

But at that moment Wasabi and the others drove up, and Hiro jumped into the safety of their car.

Yokai attacked, and after a wild chase the car plunged into the deep, dark waters of San Fransokyo Bay, but Baymax rescued Hiro and the others by floating them up to safety.

Hiro showed them a bird he had drawn. "The guy in the mask had something with this bird drawn on it. He started the fire. We have to find him."

"HIS BLOOD TYPE IS A NEGATIVE ..." said Baymax.

"You scanned him?" asked Hiro. Now they could track him by boosting Baymax's sensor! **BUT FIRST, HIRO HAD TO UPGRADE EVERYONE ...**

ビッグ・ヒーロー6

MEET BIG HERO 6!

Hiro made Baymax into a fighting, FLYING super-bot, then upgraded his friends from the lab, making amazing super-suits for them. And he created one for himself, too!

BAYMAX

BAYMAX's super-suit has
- ⭐ rocket fist
- ⭐ rocket thrusters

TAKE FLIGHT!

HIRO

HIRO's super-suit has
- ⭐ integrated computer
- ⭐ electromagnetic pads
- ⭐ tracking

CHANGE THE WORLD!

FRED

FRED's super monster-suit has
- ★ flame throwers
- ★ super bounce
- ★ sharp claws

FIRED UP!

HONEY LEMON

HONEY's super-suit has
- ★ mobile chemistry kit
for formula-making

ELEMENTS!

GO-GO

GO-GO's super-suit has
- ★ supercharged wheels
- ★ electromagnetic discs

SPEED. POWER. EDGE!

WASABI

WASABI's super-suit has
- ★ super-charged gloves
with plasma blades

BEWARE MY BLADES!

HIRO
MAKES
FRIENDS

... AND AN ENEMY, TOO!

Can you find the names of Baymax and the college lab team spelled out in the puzzle? Their names are spelled out left to right and top to bottom – but you'll have to look extra hard to find big bad Yokai's name because it's spelled out backwards.

A	Y	T	D	Q	R	C	B	I	J
G	E	A	W	A	S	A	B	I	H
H	O	N	E	Y	J	X	W	A	U
K	L	O	H	I	B	B	Y	K	V
Q	X	G	T	O	M	A	G	O	L
F	E	I	B	G	B	Y	Z	Y	E
F	R	N	C	L	I	M	O	L	M
G	O	G	O	N	G	A	R	K	O
N	A	E	Q	M	P	X	S	T	N
O	F	R	E	D	P	W	Z	V	U

WASABI
NO-GINGER
GO-GO
TOMAGO
HONEY
LEMON
FRED
BAYMAX
YOKAI

40

Answers on page 68.

SSSSSSS!

After he was attacked by the microbots, Baymax was covered in lots of tiny holes made by their sharp edges. **SSSS! SSSSS!** He had to find them all, and tape them closed before all his air escaped!

Will you help him? Look closely, and when you spot a tiny hole, draw on a piece of tape over it.

SSS!

SSSSSSS!

SSS!

SSSS!

SSSSS!

SSSSSSS!

SSSSS!

SSS!

How many pieces of tape did you draw? Write the number.

Answer on page 68.

BIG MATCH 6

Can you match the special slogans to the Big Hero 6 team members?
Write the numbers in the boxes.

GREEN BLADES OF GLORY! ☐

FLYING MAKES ME A BETTER HEALTH CARE COMPANION! ☐

FIRE-BREATHER! ☐

I LIKE SPEED! ☐

CHEMISTRY WIZARD! ☐

SUPER SMART! ☐

1

2

3

4

5

6

42

Answers on page 69.

ディズニー・アニメーション提供

モンスター映画に夢中で
コミックブックが大好きな
人当たりの良い少年が、
カギ爪をもち、火を吐き、
ものすごいジャンプをする
怪獣になります。

FRED フレッド

ディズニー・スタジオ オリジナルのアニメーション映画
お近くの映画館でご覧ください。

ビッグヒーロー6

風12号、15日に
サンフランソーキョー
に最接近へ

ゴー・ゴー・トマゴ

空手

鈴木

GO-GO

FIND THE FIERY FREDS!

Fred is a very laid-back kind of dude – until he puts on the monster-style super-suit Hiro created for him. Then he's **FIRED UP!** – so evil-doers beware! Which 2 pictures of fire-breathing Fred are exactly the same?

Answer on page 69.

CHAPTER 3

When the team was ready, "**LET'S FIND THIS GUY!**" said Hiro.

Baymax located Yokai on a small island in San Fransokyo Bay, and flew Hiro and the team there.

On the island they found an old laboratory, and activated a video. It showed Alistair Krei, the man who had tried to buy Hiro's microbots, with two teleportation portals.

"Ready for a ride, Abigail?" he asked the pilot of a space pod.

She nodded, and the pod shot into one of the portals. But – **DISASTER!** – the portal exploded and the pilot was lost inside.

As the team watched the screen, the masked man, Yokai, appeared, and commanded the microbots to attack.

"Get his neural transmitter!" Hiro told the team. "It's behind the mask!"

Hiro got the mask, but the man behind it wasn't Krei – **IT WAS PROFESSOR CALLAGHAN.** He had used the microbots to save himself from the fire!

"YOU LET TADASHI DIE?" said Hiro.

"I don't care about your brother!" Callaghan snarled.

"BAYMAX, DESTROY!" cried Hiro.

"MY PROGRAMMING PREVENTS ME FROM HARMING A HUMAN BEING," said Baymax.

Hiro opened Baymax's access port and took out the green nurse chip. That left just the red fighting chip inside.

Baymax lifted his rocket fist and aimed it at Callaghan!

"Get the nurse chip back into Baymax! Now!" Go-Go shouted.

But as the team fixed the nurse chip, Callaghan escaped. "I never should have let you help me!" Hiro told the others, and flew off on Baymax.

Hiro tried to open Baymax's access port, but the robot refused to let him, and showed Hiro a video of Tadashi with nurse chip Baymax. "You're gonna help so many people," Tadashi said.

HIRO BEGAN TO CRY. Now he understood: Tadashi had made Baymax to **HELP PEOPLE, NOT HURT THEM.**

Honey, Wasabi, Go-Go and Fred arrived with more video film evidence. They watched Krei promising Callaghan that his daughter, Abigail, would be safe. She was the lost pilot in the teleportation device!

Now they understood. "Callaghan blames Krei," Honey said.

Krei was at his company HQ when Callaghan appeared. "My daughter is gone because of you!" Callaghan yelled, as the microbots scooped up Krei and formed pillars to hold up the remaining portal. "You took everything from me. Now I am taking everything from you."

Just then Hiro arrived. "Let him go," he urged Callaghan. "This won't bring your daughter back."

But Callaghan refused to stop.

"Go for the mask!" Hiro shouted.

If they could get the neural transmitter, Callaghan could not control the microbots. "You guys! Use those big brains of yours!"

HIRO LED THEM AS A TEAM.

Soon the microbots were sucked into the portal, Baymax got Callaghan's mask, and the last microbots fell.

"**MY SENSOR IS DETECTING SIGNS OF LIFE,**" Baymax reported, pointing into the portal.

"**WHAT?**" said Hiro.

Baymax and Hiro flew into the portal and found Abigail. She was injured, but alive.

Hiro latched on to her pod, and Baymax used his rocket thrusters to move them to the exit.

But when a large chunk of debris flew towards Hiro, Baymax used his body to block it. He saved Hiro, but was hit, and his thrusters were damaged beyond repair.

"THERE IS STILL A WAY I CAN PROVIDE THE CARE YOU BOTH REQUIRE," said Baymax.

Hiro knew what that meant. "Please ... no, I need you!" Hiro shouted.

"I CANNOT DEACTIVATE UNTIL YOU SAY YOU ARE SATISFIED WITH YOUR CARE," Baymax insisted.

Hiro gulped back his tears. "I am satisfied with my care," he said, and he and Baymax HUGGED ONE LAST TIME.

Baymax used his rocket fist to get Hiro and Abigail to the exit. There was just enough power to get them to safety and as he jetted away, Hiro watched his best friend until he was too small to see.

He would never see Baymax again, but he would never forget him. NEVER.

When Hiro and Abigail crashed out of the portal, the team all looked expectantly at Hiro.

"Baymax?" Wasabi asked.

Hiro just shook his head.

That, and Hiro's sad face, told the team what they needed to know: BAYMAX WAS GONE!

Not long after, news stations reported a big story:

> A GROUP OF UNIDENTIFIED INDIVIDUALS PREVENTED
> A MAJOR CATASTROPHE. WHO ARE THESE HEROES,
> AND WHERE ARE THEY NOW?

They were at SFIT! Hiro had started classes there, in Tadashi's old work space. He put Baymax's rocket fist on his bench, the one piece of him he had been able to save. He gave it a fist bump ... and the fingers uncurled to reveal the green nurse chip! With this, **HIRO COULD REBUILD BAYMAX!**

And that's exactly what he did ...

With Baymax back, the team was complete again. If San Fransokyo needed them, **BIG HERO 6 WOULD BE READY.**

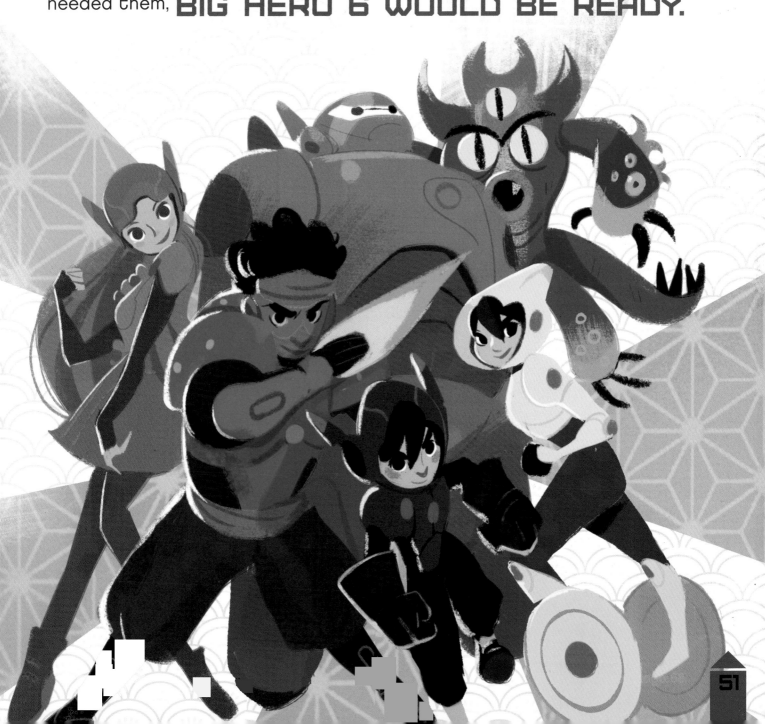

WHAT DO YOU KNOW? PART 2

Try answering these questions about the last part of the story.

1 When part of Megabot fell, what part of Hiro's body did it land on, making him cry out in pain and activating Baymax?

2 Who was the pilot of the space pod? Tick ✔ a box.

☐ **A** Annie ☐ **B** Amy ☐ **C** Abigail

3 What was the colour of the mask worn by the evil man in the long black coat?

1 ☐ and ☐

2 ☐ and ☐

3 ☐ and ☐

4 Can you make 4 words of 3 or 4 letters from the letters in

MICROBOTS

and write them on the lines?

_____

_____

_____

_____

5 The new fighting chip Hiro fitted in Baymax was yellow. True or false? Write a tick ✔ for true or a cross ✘ for false. ☐

6 Tadashi's four friends from the lab went to the warehouse to help Hiro and Baymax. Whose name is missing? Write it on the line.

HONEY   GO-GO   WASABI   _____

7 The masked man called himself Yokai. Who was he really? Tick ✔ a box.

☐ **A** Alistair Krei

☐ **B** Fred

☐ **C** Professor Callaghan

8 How did Baymax rescue the team from the submerged car? Did he

☐ **A** get them out with a fishing rod

OR

☐ **B** float them to the surface

Tick ✔ a box.

9 Baymax said,

"HIS _ _ _ _ _ _ TYPE IS _ NEGATIVE."

Can you write in the missing word and letter?

10 What did Hiro draw to show his friends? Tick ✔ a box.

☐ **A** bat   ☐ **B** bird   ☐ **C** dog

Check your answers on page 69.

ON A SCALE OF 1 TO 10, how many questions did you get right? Draw a face to show your score.

1 2 3 4 5

6 7 8 9 10

VISUAL SKILLS

Put your visual skills to the test!
Can you decide where the pieces
go to complete the picture?
Write a letter in each shape.
Hiro completed the test in under 5 minutes.
Can you match his time – or even beat it?

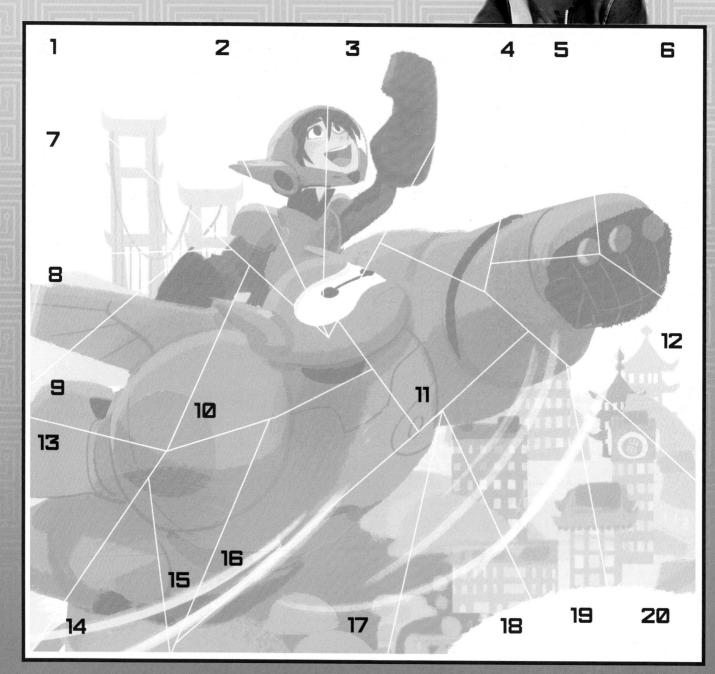

Answer on page 69.

MAKE THE MATCH

Here's a test of your observational skills! Which silhouettes match the pictures of Hiro and Go-Go?

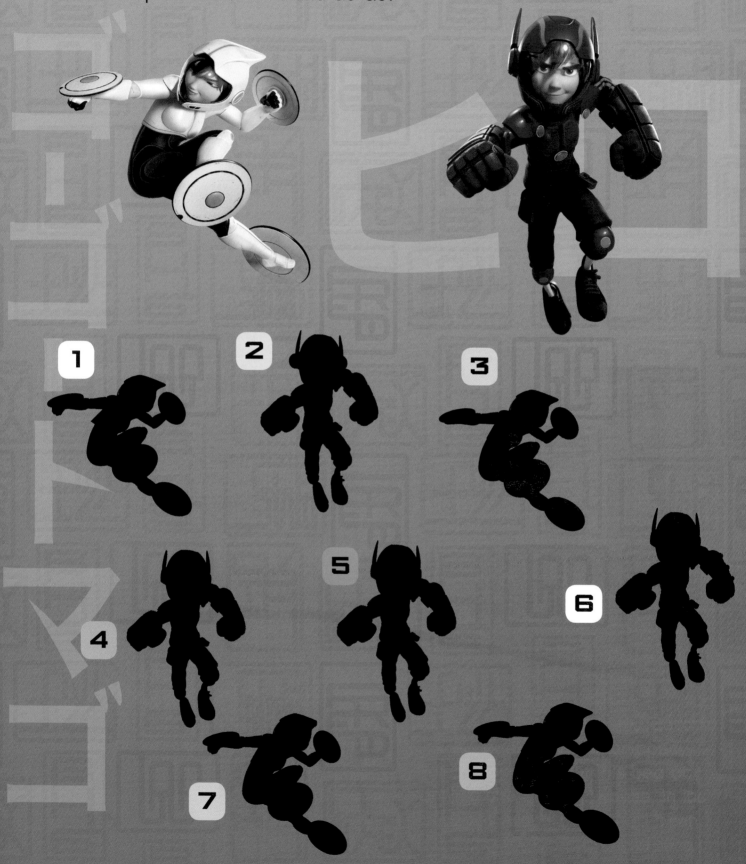

Answers on page 69.

DESIGN A BOT

Hiro spent a lot of time designing and making his super-fighting bot, **MEGABOT**. So did the bot-fight fans he pitted his bot against in robo-combat!

Use this space to design your own fight bot and give it a name. What special features will make it a winner?

NAME OF BOT ....

DESIGNED BY ....

BIG NEWS!

When Hiro and the **BIG HERO 6** team saved San Fransokyo from disaster, it was **BIG** media news!

Imagine you are the editor of the San Fransokyo Times. What will your lead front page story be? Write a powerful headline, using some of the words below. You can add a picture if you like.

HEROES　　　**CATASTROPHE**　　　**MAJOR**

DISASTER　　　**SUPER**

GROUP　　**GRATEFUL**　　**UNIDENTIFIED**

MYSTERY　　**UNKNOWN**　　**FLYING**

NUMBER MAZE

Can you find your way through the maze? Take ONLY the paths where the answer to the sums is **30**.

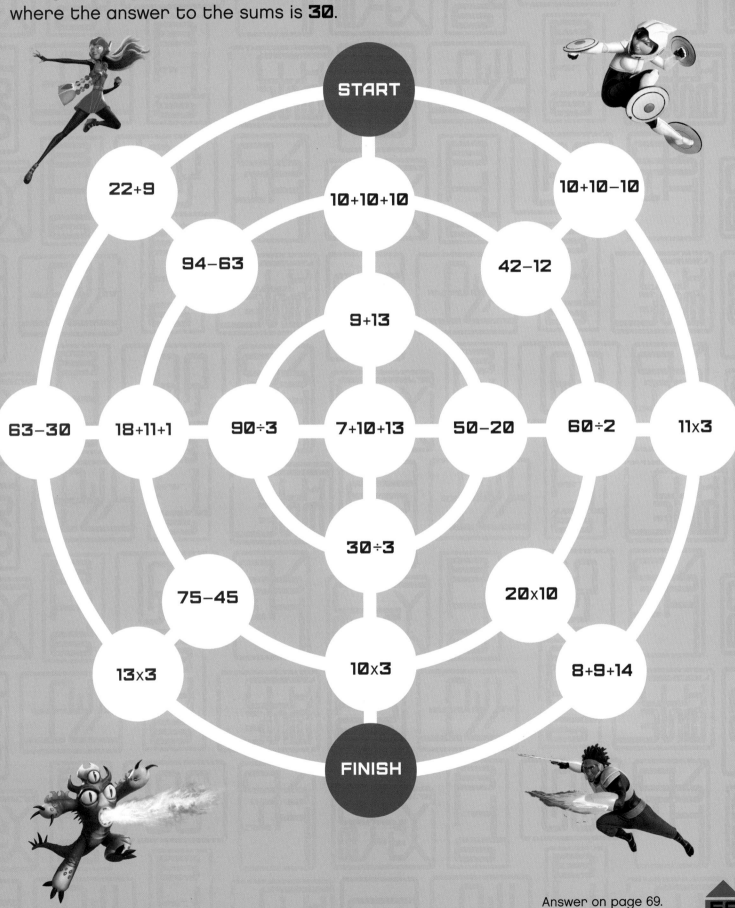

START

22+9

10+10+10

10+10-10

94-63

42-12

9+13

63-30 18+11+1 90÷3 7+10+13 50-20 60÷2 11x3

30÷3

75-45

20x10

13x3

10x3

8+9+14

FINISH

Answer on page 69.

SPOT THE
DIFFERENCE

These pictures of Hiro and the team look the same, but 10 things are different in picture 2. Take a close look – can you spot them all?

Answer on page 69.

THRUSTERS ON!

With the powerful rocket thrusters Hiro created for him, Baymax can soar across the skies over San Fransokyo – with Hiro as his passenger.

Can you guide them along the lines to his SFIT friends?

Answer on page 69.

THE MICROBOT CHALLENGE

Here's a challenge for you and a friend: which of you can collect the biggest number of microbots?

You need counters, a die and a pencil. Put your counters on **START** then take turns to roll the die. If you roll 2, move on 2 places, and so on. Keep going round the board and when you land on a **MICROBOT**, shade in one of your 12 outlines. The first to score 12 wins the challenge!

If you land on these symbols ...

SF

HAVE AN
EXTRA THROW

MISS
A TURN

6

GO ON
6 SPACES

GO BACK
4 SPACES

GO BACK
TO START

PLAYER 2 NAME

....

....

PLAYER 1 NAME

....

....

SF

SF

UNBEATABLE!

Hiro and Baymax make a great team. They are best friends who really care about each other. Copy the doodle-drawing of Hiro and Baymax, fill the page with hearts, and write your name on the line.

UNBEATABLE!
HIRO AND BAYMAX BY

BRAINIAC!

Hiro loves giving his brain a tough workout, and here's one for yours! How fast can you fill in the squares indicated by the numbers below? What do you see?

H1 H2 H5 H6 H7 H8 H9 H10 G10 F10 E10 D10 C10 B10 A10 A9 B9 C9 D9 E9 F9 G9 G8 G7 G6 F6 E6 D6 C6 B6 B7 B8 A8 A7 A6 A5 A4 A3 A2 A1 B1 C1 D1 E1 F1 G1 G2 F2 E2 D2 C2 B2 B3 B4 B5 C5 D5 E5 F5 G5

Answer on page 69.

BIG HERO 6 – PLUS 1!

How many questions did you get right in the quizzes on pages 24 and 52? Write your scores out of 10 in the boxes below and add them up.

SCORE ☐ /10   SCORE ☐ /10   TOTAL ☐ /20

Did you score more than 12 out of 20? If you did, big congrats, because that means you're a **BIG HERO 6** expert, and a real brainiac, just like Hiro! Your reward? You get to be the 7th member of the **BIG HERO 6** team, so write your details below:

TEAM NAME

....

....

SPECIAL FEATURES

....

....

....

....

SPECIAL SKILLS

....

....

....

....

Each **BIG HERO 6** team member has their own special red custom mark:

HIRO   BAYMAX   GO-GO

FRED   WASABI   HONEY

Design and draw your special custom mark.

Baymax's super-suit has red armour, Hiro's has a winged helmet, Go-Go's has yellow wheels, Fred's has three monster eyes, Wasabi's has supercharged gloves and Honey's includes a mobile chemistry kit in her shoulder bag.

Design **YOUR** BIG HERO 6 super-suit and draw it on the model.

ANSWERS

page 18 THE NEXT BIG BOT FIGHT
The next bot fight is at 7C.

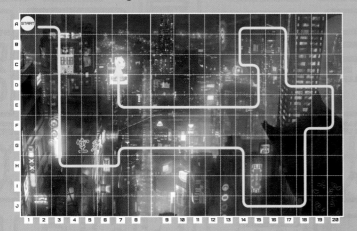

page 20 CODE BREAKER

国 米 モ ツ
ツ モ 米 国
米 ツ 国 モ
モ 国 ツ 米

page 23 SAN FRANSOKYO

A ✔ B ✔ C ✔ D ✘ E ✔ F ✘ G ✔ H ✔ I ✘

page 24 WHAT DO YOU KNOW? PART 1
1 False - he lives in San Fransokyo
2 14
3 Megabot
4 B - Tadashi
5 Robotics
6 B - San Fransokyo Institute of Technology
7 true
8 A - green
9 "HELLO, I AM BAYMAX, YOUR PERSONAL HEALTH CARE COMPANION."
10 B - headband

page 26 SAY HI TO BAYMAX
There are 33 footballs. Don't forget to count the one Baymax is playing with! The ringed ball is different.

page 28 WHAT COMES NEXT?

1 国 米 国 米 国 | 米
2 モ ツ モ ツ モ | ツ
3 器 米 国 器 米 | 国
4 ワ 戦 ヒロ ワ 戦 | ヒロ
5 器 器 器 器 器 | 器

page 40 HIRO MAKES FRIENDS

A	Y	T	D	Q	R	C	B	I	J
G	E	A	W	A	S	A	B	I	H
H	O	N	E	Y	J	X	W	A	U
K	L	O	H	I	B	B	Y	K	U
Q	X	G	T	O	M	A	G	O	L
F	E	I	B	G	B	Y	Z	Y	E
F	R	N	C	L	I	M	O	L	M
G	O	G	O	N	G	A	R	K	O
N	A	E	Q	M	P	X	S	T	N
O	F	R	E	D	P	W	Z	U	U

page 41 SSSSSSS!
There are 14 holes.

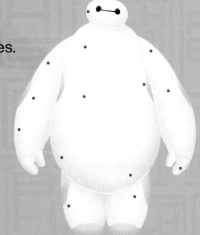